The Tortoise and the Hair

The Tortoise

by
Mark Knepprath

and the Hair

One day Puppy and Bunny

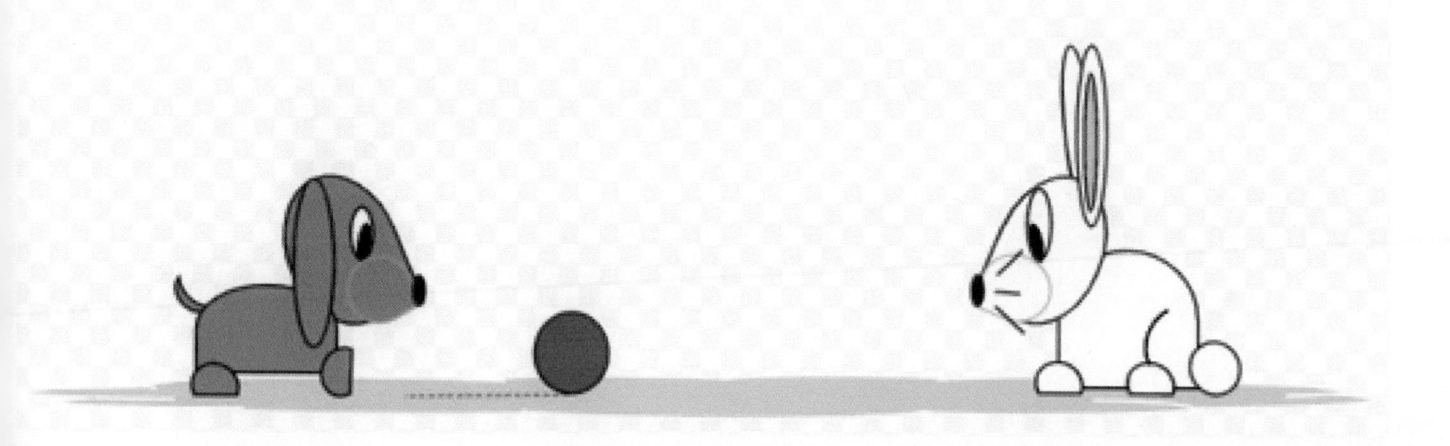

were playing in the yard...

When suddenly, the wind

blew something onto the grass.

"Ahhh! A snake!" cried Bunny.

"I don't think it's a snake,"

said Puppy. "It might be a worm."

"What should we do?" Bunny asked.

"Let's call Tortoise," said Puppy.
"He'll know what to do."

Tortoise!

"I'll be right there!"

shouted Tortoise.

Pardon me!

CRASH!!

Sorry!

Coming!

Almost there!

"Here I am," said Tortoise.

"What's the trouble?"

"Look!" said Bunny.

"A snake!"

"I don't think it's a snake,"

said Puppy. "It might be a worm."

"Well," said Tortoise,

"let's take a look."

"Hmmm...uhuh, yup,"

said Tortoise. "I see..."

"What do you see!"

cried Bunny and Puppy.

"Well," said Tortoise, "it's not

a snake, and it's not a worm..."

"What is it?"

cried Bunny and Puppy.

"It appears to be a hair!"

said Tortoise.

"Ew!" cried Bunny.

"Does it bite?"

"No," said Tortoise.

"It doesn't bite."

"What should we do with it?"

Puppy asked.

"Maybe we should comb it,"

said Tortoise.

Just then a wind came along

and blew the hair away.

"Oh well," said Tortoise...

"Hair today, gone tomorrow."

THE END

Printed in Great Britain
by Amazon